MAY ANGELI studied at the School of Arts and Crafts in Paris and later took engraving classes in Urbino, Italy. In 2013, she received the Grand Prix de l'Illustration from the Moulins Museum of Youth Illustration. *The Bear and the Duck* is her English-language debut. May lives in Paris.

For Françoise Mateu

First published in the United States in 2020
by Eerdmans Books for Young Readers,
an imprint of Wm. B. Eerdmans Publishing Co.
Grand Rapids, Michigan

www.eerdmans.com/youngreaders

Original edition copyright © 2019 Les Éditions des Éléphants, France
This edition was published by arrangement with The Picture Book Agency, France
All rights reserved

English-language translation © 2020 Eerdmans Books for Young Readers

Manufactured in China.

28 27 26 25 24 23 22 21 20   1 2 3 4 5 6 7 8 9

ISBN 978-0-8028-5555-8

A catalog record of this book is available from the Library of Congress.

Illustrations created with wood engravings.

MIX
Paper from
responsible sources
FSC® C104723
FSC
www.fsc.org

The Bear and the Duck

MAY ANGELI

EERDMANS BOOKS FOR YOUNG READERS

GRAND RAPIDS, MICHIGAN

It was the end of winter, and the day had barely started.
Duck blinked, smoothed his feathers, and stretched.
He took a running start, ready to fly off.

But his legs and wings got all tangled up,
and he rolled head over heels until—
CRASH!
He landed beak first in a jumble of branches.

The racket startled Bear from his slumber.
"What's going on?" he grumbled. "Is it spring already?"
And he went back to sleep.

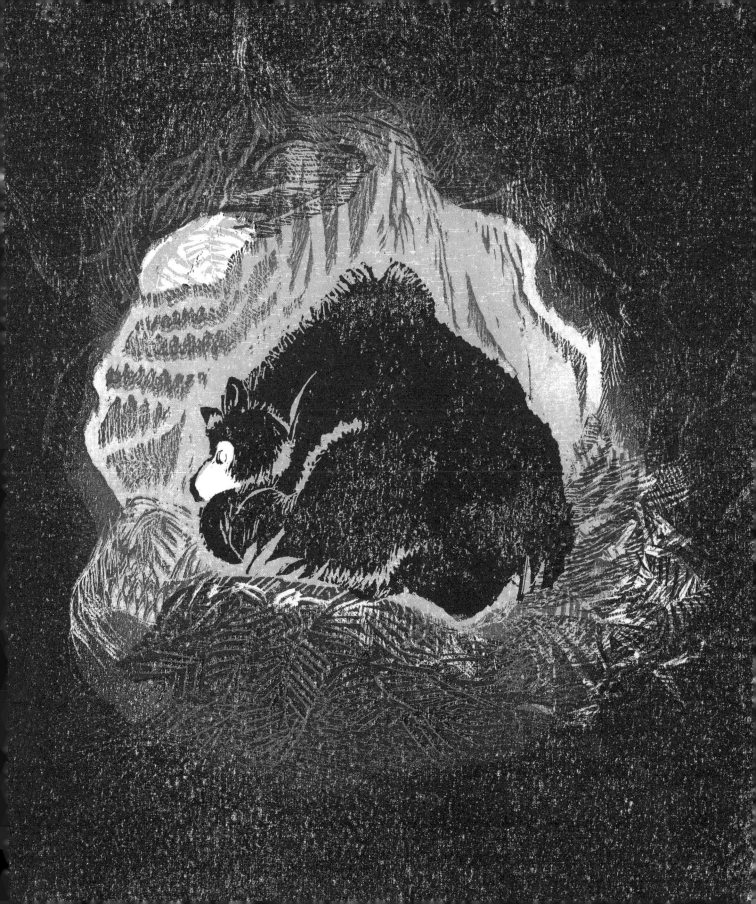

But all around him, the world was starting to thaw out.
Scowling and rather rumpled, Bear finally emerged from his den.
Duck winced in pain, but bravely called out,
"Come any closer and I'll break your head!"

Bear chuckled and shrugged his shoulders.
"Are you afraid that I'll bite you?
I'm far too old, and I don't have many teeth left."
"Then help get me out of here," Duck said, "or I'm going to pass out!"
Bear gently freed the bird and scooped him up with his big paws.
"Nothing broken, just a few scratches. We'll make you better."

"First, let's find you some shelter," Bear said.
"My den would be best."
Bear placed Duck on his old bedding.
"It's a bit messy, but it's comfortable.
Stay here and don't move," he told Duck.
"I've got some things to take care of."
After a good scratch, Bear smoothed down
his scruffy coat of fur and disappeared.

The first buds were bursting,
and from the last patches of snow,
the violets' perfume filled the air.
Bear ate some and brought some back for Duck—
who flinched when Bear placed the food in front of him.
"I'm also thirsty," Duck whimpered.
"Of course!" Bear muttered, and went to find water.

After a few days, Duck was finally
well enough to leave the den.
The two went for a walk, with Duck riding on Bear's back.
And while Bear bathed, Duck splashed around.
Sometimes, lying in the grass,
Duck would puff up his chest and start a story . . .

He would tell stories about escaping fearsome hunters
and flying past mountains that stretched up to touch the moon.
Bear would grunt, admiring Duck's stories,
or listen with one ear as he dozed.

Then one day, it happened.
"I feel really good," Duck said.
"I think I can leave now . . . "

He raised his beak to the sky,
where the other birds were waiting for him.
"Thank you, Bear! I'll see you soon. Don't worry—I'll be back."
And after a few stretches, Duck took off.

With Duck gone,
the days seemed empty.
Bear missed his friend.
He ate, even though he wasn't hungry.

Then came the icy winds and the first snow.
Just like every year before, Bear settled into his den.
"I may never see Duck again.
But I guess that's life, as they say when sad things happen."
And Bear fell asleep for the long winter.

Bear woke up to the sound of a dove singing:
"It's spring!"
He stepped outside, scratched his stiff body,
and decided to have a bath.
"What a fleabag!" he thought to himself.

Bear ate some grass.
Then, warmed by the first rays of sun,
he lay down and closed his eyes.
Like in a dream, a quack-quack
echoed in his head.

That's when he heard a voice in his ear:
"Come on! Get up, old Bear! It's me—I'm back!"
"It's about time," Bear replied grumpily.
Duck stroked Bear's head.
They sat side by side.
"I have so many things to tell you—" Duck began.
"But no, you go first!"